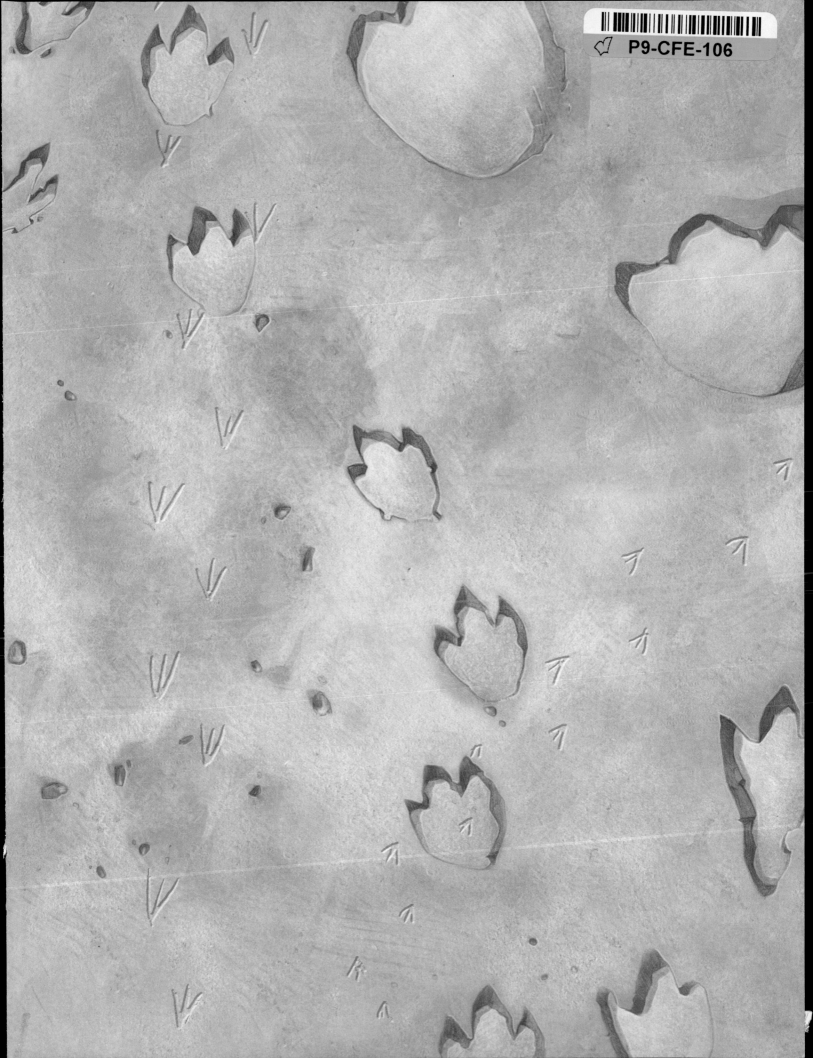

To all the GREAT children's lit people in the Bay Area—
especially Sharon Levin, the Rondbergs, Valerie Lewis,
Monica Holmes, and everyone else at Hicklebees;
everyone at the Reading Bug; and our local SCBWIs. —T. M.

For Ali, my little dino. —M. P.

STERLING CHILDREN'S BOOKS
New York

An Imprint of Sterling Publishing
387 Park Avenue South
New York, NY 10016

STERLING CHILDREN'S BOOKS and the distinctive Sterling Children's Books logo
are trademarks of Sterling Publishing Co., Inc.

Text © 2013 by Tim Myers
Illustrations © 2013 by Macky Pamintuan
Designed by Elizabeth Phillips

ISBN 978-1-4027-7798-1

Library of Congress Cataloging-in-Publication Data

Myers, Tim.
  Down at the Dino Wash Deluxe / by Tim Myers ; illustrated by Macky Pamintuan.
     p. cm.
  Summary: Dinosaurs from a finicky stegosaurus and a knobby old ankylosaur to the frightening tyrannosaurus rex
get washed and shined at the Dino Wash Deluxe. Includes section with facts about the dinosaurs mentioned
in the story.
  ISBN 978-1-4027-7798-1 (hc-plc with jacket : alk. paper) [1. Dinosaurs--Fiction. 2. Cleanliness--Fiction.]
I. Pamintuan, Macky, ill. II. Title.
  PZ7.M9918Do 2012
  [E]--dc22
2010020713

Distributed in Canada by Sterling Publishing
c/o Canadian Manda Group, 165 Dufferin Street
Toronto, Ontario, Canada M6K 3H6
Distributed in the United Kingdom by GMC Distribution Services
Castle Place, 166 High Street, Lewes, East Sussex, England BN7 1XU
Distributed in Australia by Capricorn Link (Australia) Pty. Ltd.
P.O. Box 704, Windsor, NSW 2756, Australia

For information about custom editions, special sales, and premium and corporate purchases,
please contact Sterling Special Sales at 800-805-5489 or specialsales@sterlingpublishing.com.

Manufactured in China

Lot #:
2 4 6 8 10 9 7 5 3 1
10/12
www.sterlingpublishing.com/kids

DOWN AT THE DINO WASH DELUXE

by **TIM MYERS**

Illustrated by **MACKY PAMINTUAN**

STERLING CHILDREN'S BOOKS
New York

Welcome to the
DINO WASH DELUXE!

How's a dinosaur supposed to stay clean in the city?

We soap 'em, scrub 'em, then send 'em down the line for rinsing and drying.

But this job's no picnic—you gotta know the customers! No two dinos are alike, and they all need scrub-a-dubbing.

Our first customer of the day is **Ankylosaurus**. Ever count all the knobs and spikes on this dusty old guy? We wash every last one.

Styracosaurus rolls in next. He's plenty of work too. Oh, he's great—but with that frill and those wicked horns, it takes an hour to get him shiny!

After his scrub-down, Ankylosaurus tells me, "Just wanted to warn ya, kid— **Tyrannosaurus rex** is in town."

Whoa! That's news to me! *Bad* news.
The T. rex has never come in before—
and he's one serious meat-eater!

But there's no time to worry about that now. I've got work to do.

Pachycephalosaurus is next in line. He's as bald as Mr. Shinetop, my principal. I climb a ladder to rinse him.

And I love hosing down **Quetzalcoatlus**.
Sometimes she sneaks a beakful and
douses me!

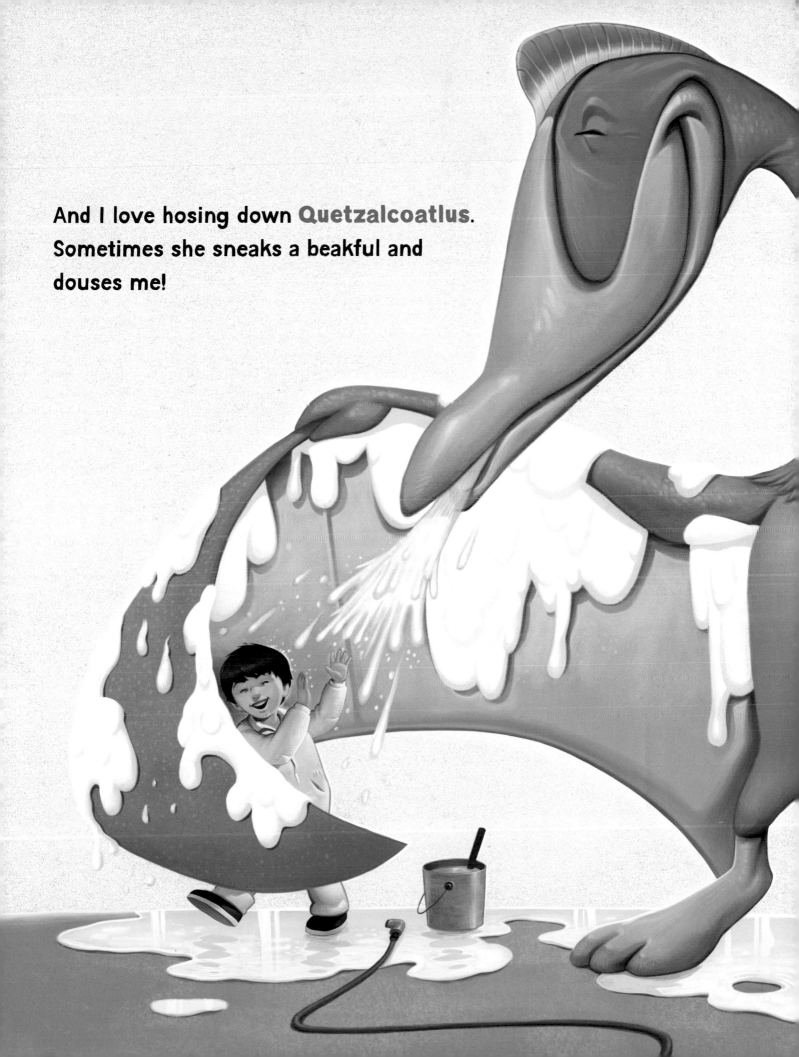

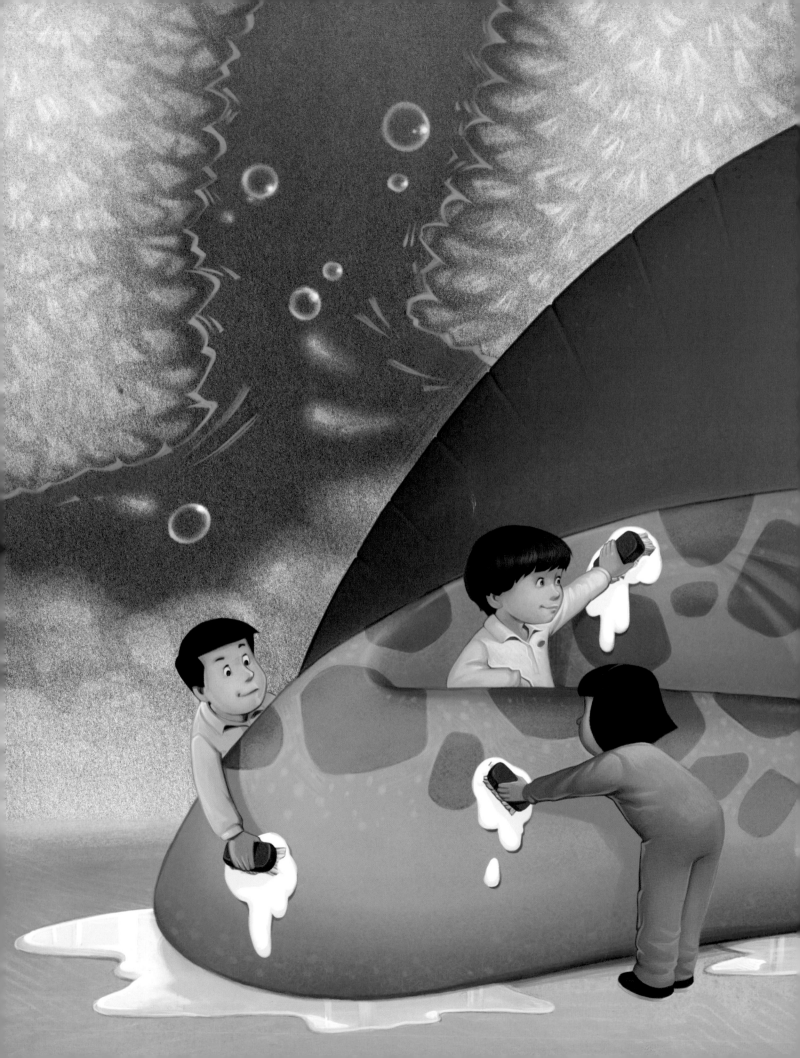

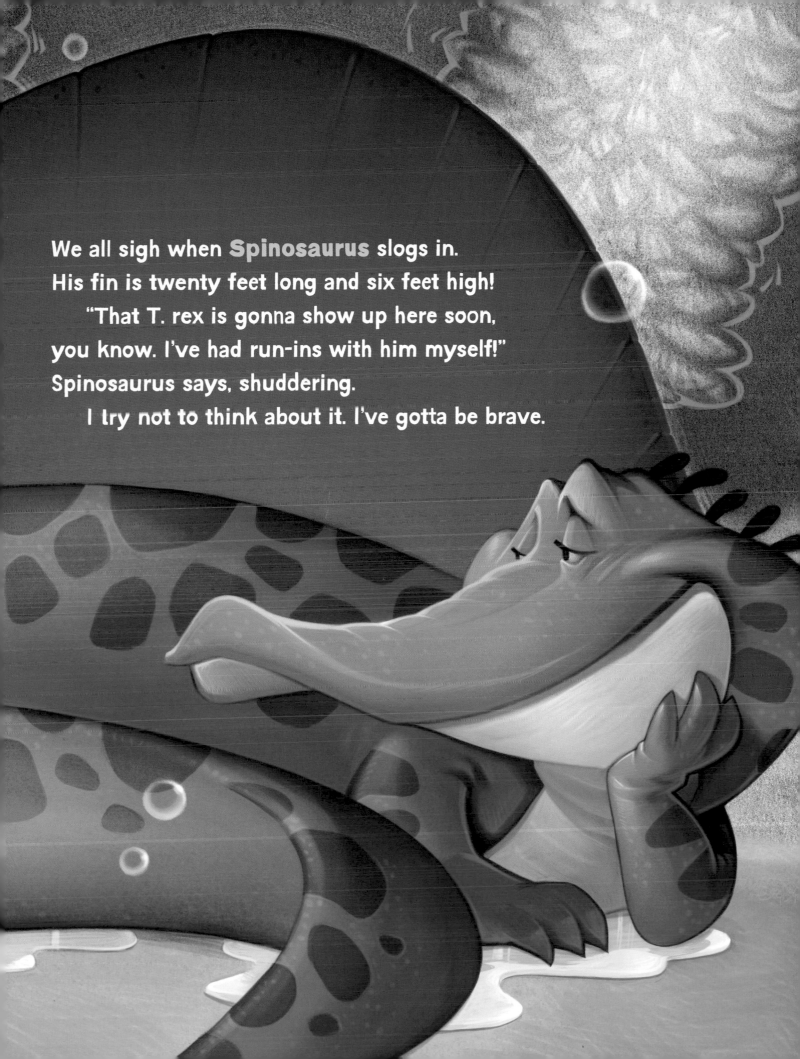

We all sigh when **Spinosaurus** slogs in.
His fin is twenty feet long and six feet high!
   "That T. rex is gonna show up here soon,
you know. I've had run-ins with him myself!"
Spinosaurus says, shuddering.
   I try not to think about it. I've gotta be brave.

Stegosaurus is finicky about his fins.

"Make 'em clean as dinner plates!" he orders.

Yikes! What if T. rex wants ME on a dinner plate?

It'll be okay, I tell myself.

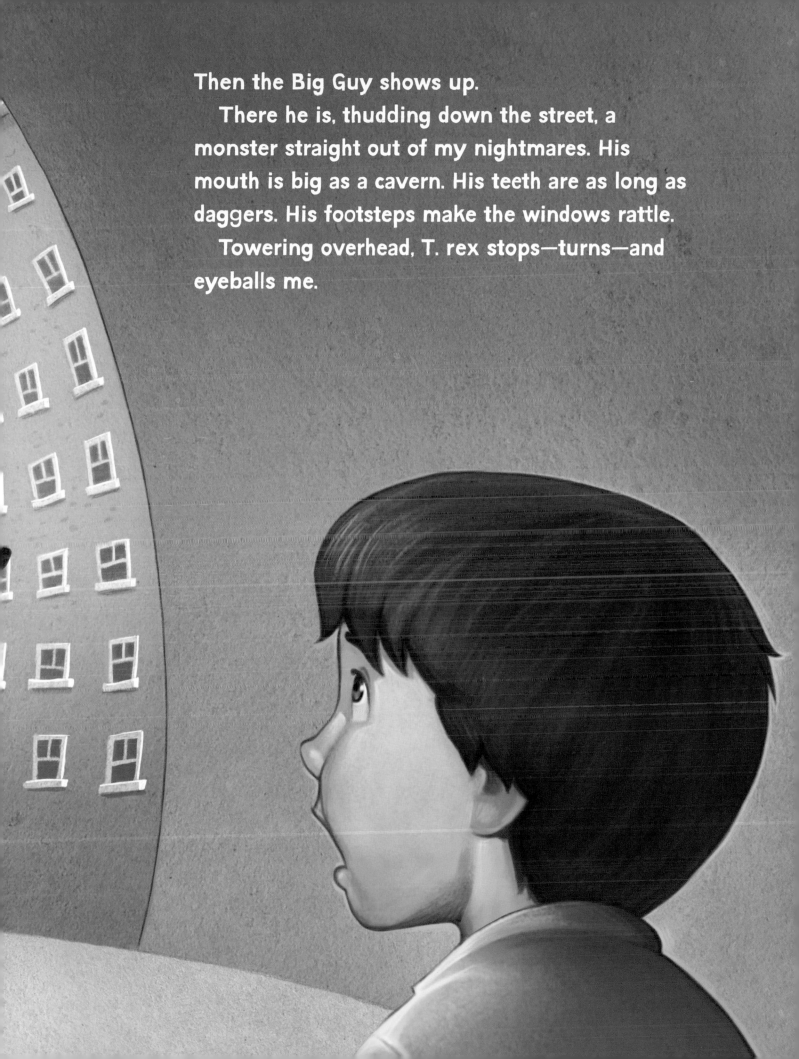

Then the Big Guy shows up.

There he is, thudding down the street, a monster straight out of my nightmares. His mouth is big as a cavern. His teeth are as long as daggers. His footsteps make the windows rattle.

Towering overhead, T. rex stops—turns—and eyeballs me.

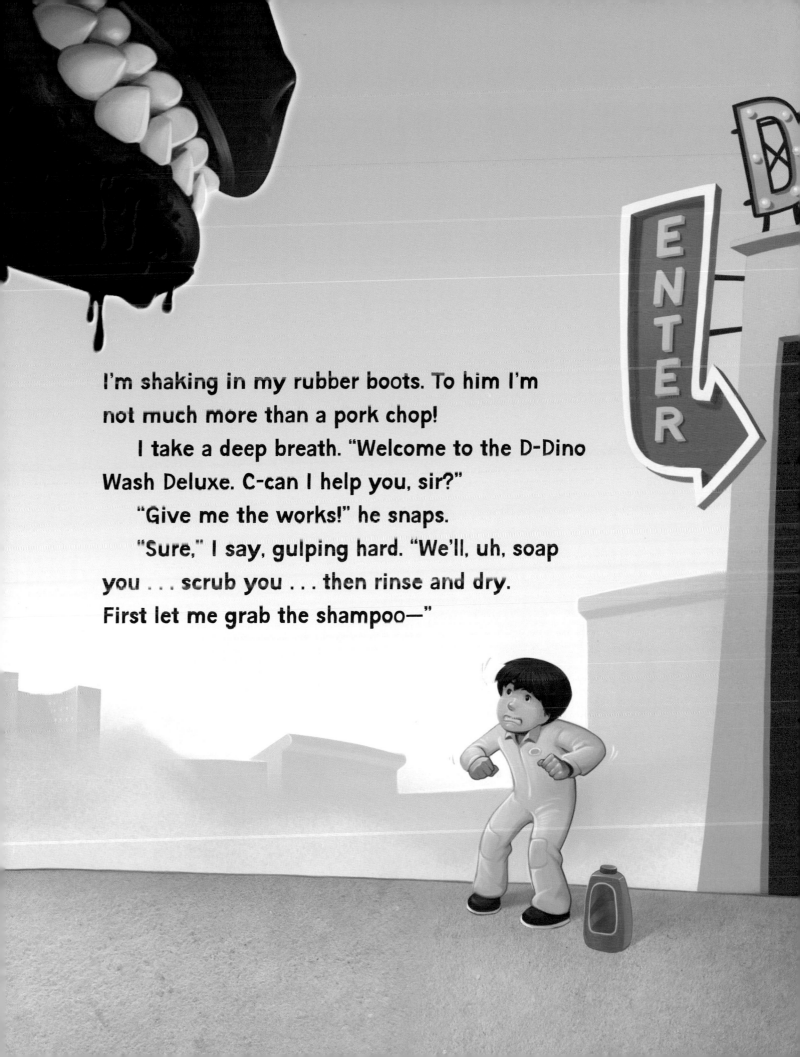

I'm shaking in my rubber boots. To him I'm
not much more than a pork chop!

I take a deep breath. "Welcome to the D-Dino
Wash Deluxe. C-can I help you, sir?"

"Give me the works!" he snaps.

"Sure," I say, gulping hard. "We'll, uh, soap
you . . . scrub you . . . then rinse and dry.
First let me grab the shampoo—"

ENTER

He leans in closer, glaring at the shampoo bottle
I'm holding.

"You're not going to use THAT, are you?"
he growls.

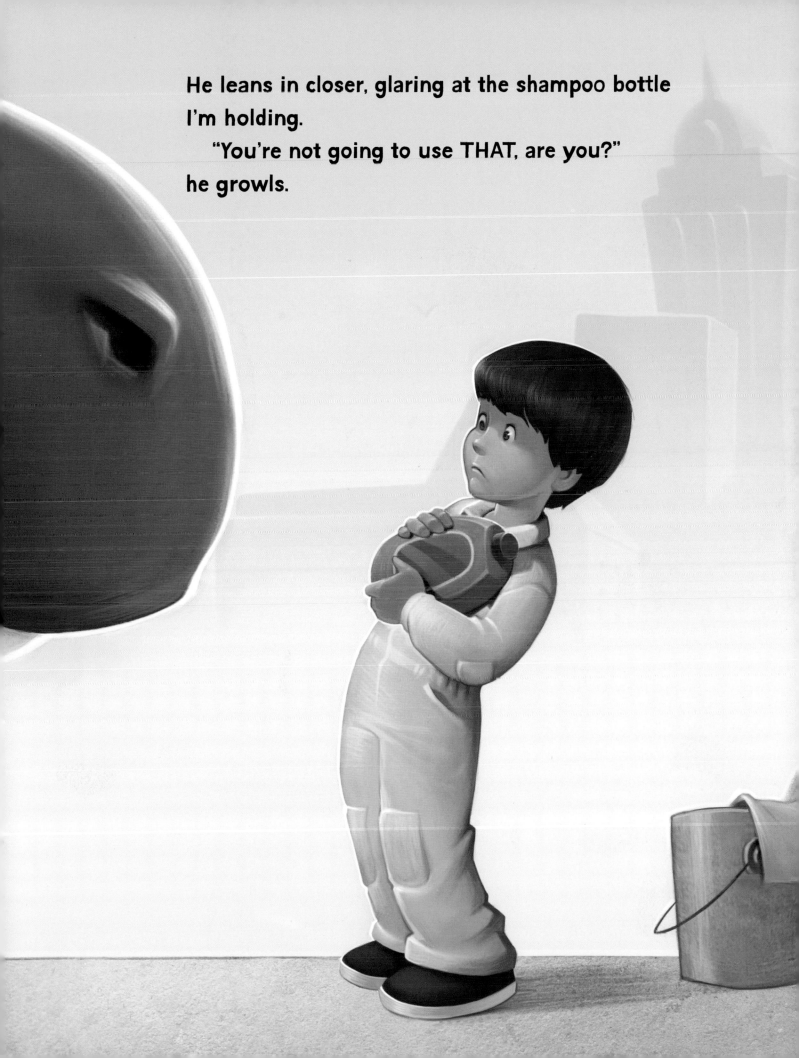

"It stings," he whimpers.

Suddenly, I know just what to do.

"Don't worry. I used to be afraid of that too," I whisper to him.

"Really?" he says.

"Totally! But we do things right at the Dino Wash Deluxe. I won't get a speck of soap in those peepers!"

Sure enough, I clean him up in a jiffy.
Soap him, scrub him, send him down the line.

And afterward—he's
just so proud of himself!

Ever since that day, T. rex has been a perfect
gentleman. Now I even scrub his back choppers.
    You know what? I LOVE working at the Dino Wash Deluxe!
It's a job-asaurus!

Ankylosaurus (an-KIE-luh-SORE-us)
This dinosaur, with huge knobs on its tail, rows of spikes on its sides, and bony plates all over its body, had its own personal armor—which must have made it feel safe when it went for a walk!

Spinosaurus (SPINE-uh-SORE-us)
Its name means "spiny lizard." This dinosaur is most famous for the huge sail or spiny fin on its back, which could grow up to six feet high. Talk about a mohawk!

Tyrannosaurus rex (tie-RAN-oh-SORE-us-reks)
Everybody knows T. rex. But did you know that it could bite off 500 pounds at once?

Stegosaurus (STEG-uh-SORE-us) Its name means "roofed lizard." Stegosaurus's neck, back, and tail carried two rows of bony plates, and its tail was covered with spikes. It could grow as big as a bus! Scientists believe it used those spikes to protect itself—ouch!

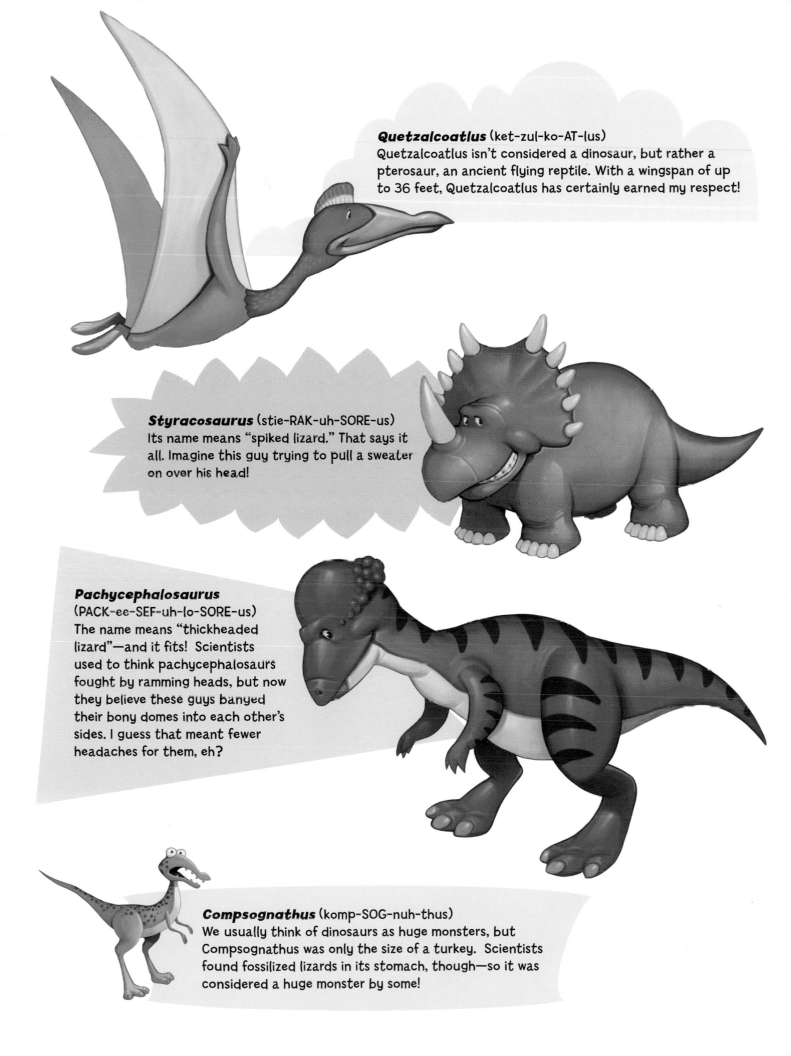

Quetzalcoatlus (ket-zul-ko-AT-lus)
Quetzalcoatlus isn't considered a dinosaur, but rather a pterosaur, an ancient flying reptile. With a wingspan of up to 36 feet, Quetzalcoatlus has certainly earned my respect!

Styracosaurus (stie-RAK-uh-SORE-us)
Its name means "spiked lizard." That says it all. Imagine this guy trying to pull a sweater on over his head!

Pachycephalosaurus
(PACK-ee-SEF-uh-lo-SORE-us)
The name means "thickheaded lizard"—and it fits! Scientists used to think pachycephalosaurs fought by ramming heads, but now they believe these guys banged their bony domes into each other's sides. I guess that meant fewer headaches for them, eh?

Compsognathus (komp-SOG-nuh-thus)
We usually think of dinosaurs as huge monsters, but Compsognathus was only the size of a turkey. Scientists found fossilized lizards in its stomach, though—so it was considered a huge monster by some!

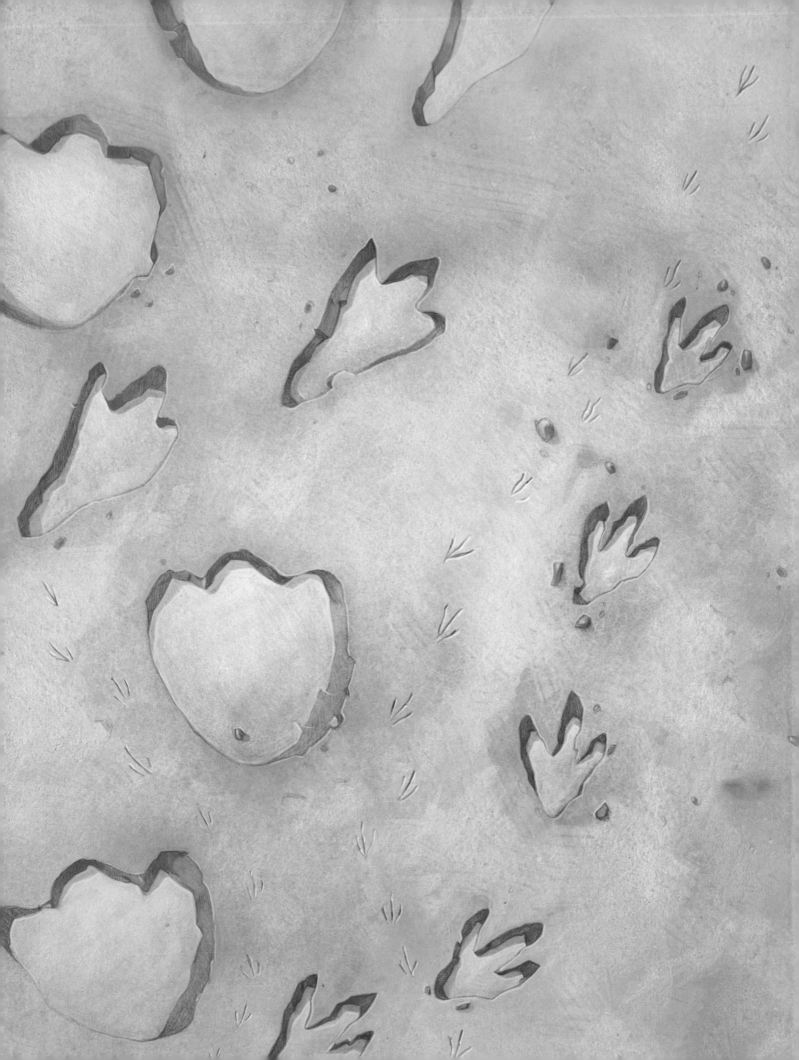